LOST IN THE FOREST

By Richard D. Schwerman

Illustrated by Richard Wahl

 CHILDRENS PRESS, CHICAGO

Dedication

To children everywhere.
May life continue to be an exciting
adventure for you. It is you know.

God loves you—everyone
and so do I.

RDS

Library of Congress Cataloging in Publication Data

Schwerman, Richard D
  Lost in the forest.

  SUMMARY: While searching for their lost dog in
the forest, Susan and her brother have a chance to
learn something about forestry from the forester
who helps them.
  [1. Forests and forestry—Fiction] I. Wahl,
Richard, 1939-   II. Title.
PZ7.S41264Lo   [Fic]   75-35938
ISBN 0-516-03522-3

1 2 3 4 5 6 7 8 9 10 11 12 R 78 77 76

CONTENTS

Chapter 1

SPRING CLEAN-UP AND
A CHASE

"Please hurry, Tom," said Susan. "Aunt Martha wants us home before five o'clock."

"I have to fix the leash, don't I," answered Tom as he wrapped another turn of wire around the leather strap. "Why do we have to take Skipper anyway?"

"Oh Tom! Skipper has never walked through a forest before, and besides I already told him he could go," said Susan patting Skipper. "Haven't I, boy?"

"There, it is all fixed," said Tom. "Hook him up while I get my fly rod and bait box."

"We're leaving, Aunt Martha," shouted Tom. "We'll be back in about two hours. The boats are all down at the shore, washed out and turned over. Uncle Max is out trying one of the motors."

"Now stay on the logging trail," said Aunt Martha, "and keep Skipper on the leash. Spring is a bad time for a dog to run loose in the woods."

"Okay, we'll be careful," said Susan half running and half falling after Skipper.

Tom and Susan, along with their parents Ralph and Dorothy Jensen, were helping their aunt and uncle open their resort for the summer. The Schuberts' Trails End Resort was a lovely, little place, nestled on the east shore of Merkel Lake. The Schuberts' guests were mostly fishermen, and because the lake joined the Turtle and the Flambeau flowages, they were very busy during the fishing season.

Except for another resort about one mile away and some private cabins scattered along the flowages, Trails End was surrounded by nothing but forests and water.

"Tom, if the fishing season doesn't open until this Saturday, why are you taking your fishing stuff to Sand Lake?" asked Susan.

"Pan fish, Sue," replied Tom. "The season opens Saturday on walleyes, northern, and all other game fish except muskies, but the season for pan fish is always open. Uncle Max says that Sand Lake is tops for them."

Tom, Susan, and Skipper walked down the driveway to the county road, crossed it, and entered the old Logging Road. Years ago this road had been used to drag timber out of the forest. The narrow road turned and twisted through the forest. If followed to its end, the road would lead about five miles into the woods. It passed the north edge of Sand Lake about a mile in, just where a small creek emptied into the lake.

Tom and Susan were walking silently down the trail. Both were fascinated by the beauty of the trees and shrubs springing back to life after a winter's sleep.

"Remember how beautiful the trees were last fall when we were up here?" asked Susan.

"Everything seems so bare now," answered Tom. "Look, Sue, the maples are just starting to bud. Do you see the red shoots coming out of the branches?"

"Yes, it seems so strange to be able to see so far into the woods," Susan added. "Last summer you couldn't see more than twenty feet from the logging road."

Suddenly Tom began to whistle loudly what seemed to be a hodgepodge of notes.

"What's that for?" asked Susan, somewhat annoyed.

"Well, Uncle Max said we should make a lot of noise when we walk in the forest at this time of the year," answered Tom. "Most animals are out walking their young ones now and don't like people near. We should sort of warn them we're coming."

"Hey, Sue, look at Skipper!" Tom cried. Skipper had stopped dead and was staring into the underbrush on the left side of the road. He was making a soft growling sound in his throat.

"What's the matter, boy?" asked Susan. "Tom, what does he see?"

"I don't know," answered Tom, "but something just moved in that clump of evergreen over there. Look! It's a deer!"

Suddenly from the group of young spruce trees jumped a doe, its white tail straight up in the air.

Skipper raced after the deer, leash and all.

"Why did you let the dog go?" Tom asked Susan excitedly.

"I didn't let him go! I'm still holding the end of his leash! It was your great repair job!" cried Susan.

"Well, you made me hurry," answered Tom.

"Here, Skipper! Here, Skipper!" Susan shouted. "Skipper, come back! Oh, Tom, what are we going to do?"

"Search me. Just keep calling, I guess. He'll come back," said Tom. "I don't see him anymore, but I can hear him barking off to the north. Sue, I think the deer is leading him back toward the county road. Wait! Quiet now."

After a long pause, he said "Sue, I don't hear Skipper anymore."

Chapter 2

THE MAN WITH A PAINT CAN

Susan looked at Tom with tears in her eyes. "I'm scared," she said. "Suppose Skipper can't find his way back? What if he follows the deer deep into the forest? He's only a puppy, Tom, six months old. He won't know how to find his way out. Should we run and tell Uncle Max? Maybe if...."

"Hold it! Hold it!" Tom stopped her. "Let's just stay here a while. Skipper is a hunting dog, isn't he? He should be able to smell out his own trail back to here. Anyway I know the deer will be back. Look in here, Sue, but walk slowly and quietly."

Susan peered into the brush where Tom was standing and cried, "Oh, how beautiful! A baby fawn! May I pet it or hold it? How did you ever see it? It is almost invisible there in the brush."

"Better not go any farther," Tom said. "Its mother probably told it to stay put and that's just what it should do. Remember Dad said never to touch a wild animal for any reason."

"Wait." Suddenly Tom put his hand on Susan's shoulder. "Sue, look way out in the forest in the direction I'm pointing. Do you see anything?"

Susan took a long, careful look. Then, turning to Tom, she said, "I don't see anything. Did you see Skipper?"

"No, it wasn't that. I'm not sure Sue, but I thought I saw a man walking out there. He seemed to go from behind one tree to another. There! There he goes again. Just on top of that hill over there. Look. He's got a yellow hat on. He's doing something to the trees."

"Oh yes, Tom, I see him too! Let's go over and ask if he'll help find Skipper."

"Oh, no," answered Tom. "We're not to go away from the trail. Remember? Look. He seems to be walking out toward the county road now. Let's run down to the road and see if we can reach him before he leaves. He must have his car there someplace."

They reached the road just as a green pickup truck went by.

"Do you suppose that's the man?" asked Susan.

"No. He didn't have time to get to the road yet. Here. You take my rod and tackle and I'll run ahead. He must be parked around that curve."

Tom raced around the curve and reached a yellow pickup just as a man with a yellow hat came from the trees.

"Hi! Out jogging?" the man asked. "Nice day for it."

"No," answered Tom "I was trying to reach you before you left." He introduced himself and told the man what had happened. As he finished, Susan arrived.

"This is my sister Susan," said Tom.

"My name is Dick Russell," the man said. "I'm Senior Forester with the Industrial Forest's Corporation. How can I help?"

"We were hoping you'd help us find Skipper, Mr. Russell," Tom answered. "We don't know how to start. Did you see him when he took after that deer?"

"Sure did. I was wondering how a nice young springer spaniel like that got loose in these woods. Bad time of the year for that."

"Yes, we know," Susan answered. "He got away from me when the leash broke."

"That's too bad, Susan," said Dick. "We'll find Skipper, but I'm afraid we may have a problem doing it."

"Why's that?" Tom asked.

"Well, when that doe passed me she was really traveling and leading Skipper on a zigzag course. The last I saw of them they crossed this road at the next bend down there. I'm afraid the doe was heading for the dike across to Big Island."

"Why is Big Island such a problem?" questioned Tom.

"Because it is just what the name says, Tom," answered Dick. "It has more than fifty square miles of forests, marsh, pot holes, and heavy underbrush. If the doe wants to lose Skipper, that's where she will do it. There are only a few old logging trails on Big Island, and most are grown over. Unless you swim, there's only one way on or off."

"What should we do?" asked Tom.

"First let's go to Trails End and let your parents know what happened."

"Mom and Dad are not there," Tom said. "They're in Ironwood. We don't expect them back until after supper."

"We'll let Max and Martha know then. Put your gear in the back of the truck and we'll get started."

"Before we go, may I ask you something?" questioned Susan.

"Go right ahead, Sue. What do you want to know?"

"What were you doing to the trees back there in the forest?"

"I was painting them, Sue," answered Dick.

"Painting them?" Susan said.

"That's right—with these spray paints. I was marking the trees our company will be removing later this year. Let's go now and tell your aunt and uncle about Skipper," said Dick as he climbed into the truck.

Chapter 3

LOST ON BIG ISLAND

"Hi, Max," shouted Dick Russell. "It's good to see you back. Are you ready for the invasion this weekend?"

"I'm almost ready. There's just one shower drain to fix in cabin number three," said Max, pointing to the cabin nearest the lake. "What was Skipper barking at before, Susan? I heard him down at the lake. He sounded excited."

Susan told her uncle what had happened. Dick added the part about the deer heading for the Big Island dike.

"I think you're right about the deer heading for Big Island. For a while I heard the barking coming from that direction. I thought it was just echoes. What do you think we should do, Dick?" asked Uncle Max.

"Well," said the forester. "I have some men working with a survey crew on the west side of the island. Why don't we drive over there now and try to call the dog in. If we don't find him now, we'll tell Red and Ira, my cutting crew over there, to keep an eye out for him tomorrow."

"Tomorrow!" cried Susan. "Do you mean Skipper will be in that forest all night?"

"It's possible, Susan," Max said. "But let's not think about that until we've looked for him. Can we go over in your truck, Dick? My pickup has a starter out."

"Sure thing, Max," answered the forester. "I

have the crew truck with the big cab. Tom and Susan can sit in the pull-down seats back of the front seat."

All four walked up from the lake to where the truck was parked. Uncle Max told Aunt Martha where they were going and why. He asked her to hold supper and said that they would be back in about an hour and a half.

"If Ralph and Dorothy get back from Ironwood before we do, tell them what we're up to," Max added as he walked out the door of the main ledge.

They all climbed into the truck. The forester was driving and Uncle Max was sitting beside him. Tom and Susan sat in back.

They drove to the county road, turned left and drove north about half a mile until they reached a narrow road that cut through the forest to their left. They took this road until they reached the dike.

The dike actually was a land fill that stretched out from the mainland across to Big Island. It separated the Turtle Flowage from Merkle Lake. Near the center of the dike there was a large tunnel or culvert. Boats used this to pass between the two waters. On top of the dike was laid a gravel road some ten to twelve feet wide. It had

been used many years before to haul cut timber out from the island and would soon be so used again. In the meantime, the dike was used mostly by hikers or hunters heading for Big Island and back.

As the road entered the island it became just tire ruts winding their way through the trees and underbrush. About three hundred yards in, the road made a fork. One trail headed south toward the center of the island and the other headed west.

"I'm going to drive over to see Red and Ira first," said Dick "They may have seen the dog. Besides, they will be going home soon, and we should talk to them before they leave."

They took the right fork and began driving
slowly on the three-mile, twisting, turning road
to the place where the survey crew was working.

"Mr. Russell," said Susan. "Why are these
people working out here? What are they sur-
veying?"

"Sue," he answered, "they're marking the
boundary lines of the land my company owns.
The company owns much of the land on Big Island. However, other industrial firms own land
on the island and the state owns all of the central
part. We will be cutting timber on the island this
winter, and we're marking the boundaries so
that the cutters and loggers stay on our own
property."

"Does your company own the woods we saw you in this morning?" asked Tom.

"No, Tom," answered the forester. "That land belongs to your uncle's neighbor. Our company has the contract to cut timber on that land. The forest is too dense and too dark. He wants to thin out the old and dying trees so that the young growth can take hold and grow. More people who own forest land should do that. They'd have a much healthier forest."

Max suddenly pointed ahead. "Look! A black bear with cubs," he said.

The forester slowed the truck to a crawl.

Susan peered out the side window in the direction her uncle was pointing. "One, two—three cubs. Uncle Max, isn't that a lot of cubs?" she asked.

"Yes, Susan," answered her uncle. "One or two is the usual number. I've seen four, but that is very rare."

Quickly the bear herded her cubs into the underbrush and out of sight.

They continued on toward the west for about half a mile. There they came upon another pick-up truck and a jeep station wagon. Four men were gathered around the pickup truck, looking at a large map spread out on the hood.

The forester pulled his truck next to the men and stopped. "Hi, Red, Ira," he said. "Through for the day?"

"Through period," the red-haired man said, pointing south. "The survey crew is just packing up. All the section lines are cleared and marked. It's all set for the winter. Here's the section map. All the drag trails we cleared are marked. All the lines check out, Dick."

Mr. Russell introduced everyone and then told the crew about Skipper and the deer.

Ira looked at Susan and said, "I saw your dog, Susan. It must have been about an hour ago. That doe was leading him into the marsh just south of that big yellow birch stand. She'll lose him there because there must be a foot of water standing in those tamaracks. Skipper is going to be one tired pup."

The surveyors had to leave for they had a long drive. They said good-bye and promised that they would look for the dog on the way out.

Chapter 4

THE SEARCH

As the surveyor's jeep pulled away, Red turned to the forester and said, "Dick, why don't you leave Tom with us. We'll go back to where Ira saw the dog and try to call him in. The rest of you can go back and take that left trail to the other side of the marsh and see if you can find him there."

"Sounds good," answered the forester. "Then we can all work our way back and meet at the fork. If we don't find Skipper by six-thirty, Susan, I think we should call it off until morning."

"I understand," Susan said. "Maybe we'll find him on the other side."

The forester, Max, and Susan climbed into the truck and slowly drove away. Red, Ira, and Tom began walking south along the cleared survey line.

"Skipper followed the deer into the marsh just where those rocks stick out of that big mound," said Ira. "See it? It's the hill with that lone big birch right on top."

"I see it," Red answered. "Tom and I will go down there and call the dog. You stay here and keep an eye and ear open. I think you have the best view of the marsh right here."

"Get to it," Ira answered as he settled down on top of a large boulder. Lighting his pipe and taking several puffs, he looked at Tom and smiled. "Time's a-wasting," he said and looked out over the marsh.

Red and Tom began their walk down to the spot Ira indicated. Tom began calling loud and clear, "Skipper! Here Skipper! Skipper!"

Meanwhile, the truck had reached the southern side of the marsh. The three searchers were too far from the others to hear Tom calling. Except for a gentle breeze whispering through the needles of some close-by white pines and the calls of some far-off crows, everything was silent.

The road or trail seemed to end here on the high ground overlooking the marsh. The land was clear, more like a meadow. Some young trees had grown here and there, but it was mostly grass and brush. On the far side of the clearing the ruins of old buildings stuck out of the brush.

"This was an old logging camp, Sue," said Dick. "Sixty or seventy years ago this was a busy place. Now, during the summer, campers

stay right where we're standing. Sometimes
hunters stay here in the fall.''

"Susan," said her uncle, "why don't you call
Skipper a few times. Then we'll all be quiet
and see if we can hear anything. I'm going to
walk over to the other side of that hill. I'll have a
good view of the part we can't see from here.''

Susan began calling. She stopped to listen, but
not a sound could be heard from the marsh.

After calling and listening for about twenty
minutes, Susan turned to the forester, who was
looking through binoculars he had taken from
the truck.

"Mr. Russell," she said, "Do you do anything besides paint trees?"

Taken by surprise by the question, he began to laugh.

"Excuse me for laughing, Sue," he said, "But your question surprised me. Actually, marking trees for cutting is just a very small part of the work I do. As Senior Forester I manage all the forest land holdings my company owns in several counties in Wisconsin and Upper Michigan. We call it the Ironwood Management area."

"Do you have many men working for you, Mr. Russell?" Susan asked.

"Not really, Sue," answered the forester. "When the company wants to cut over a section of our forest lands, we let out contracts to private cutters and loggers. They cut, trim, stack, and haul the logs to the various markets. You see, Sue, our company does not use all the trees it cuts. We only use the trees that make good pulpwood for our paper plant in Tomahawk. The other trees, such as some pine species and hardwoods like white and yellow birch and maples, are sent to various sawmills. There they will be cut for use as building and crating lumber, plywood, furniture, and other specialties."

"Mr. Russell, don't you hurt the forest when you cut trees out of it? I've seen some places where all the trees were cut down. Will those woods ever grow back?"

"Sue, when you see a section of land that is completely cut over, it is generally hardwood stands or aspen. These trees grow very thick and generally very fast. They are harvested by clear cutting when they mature, because the entire floor of the woods is already reseeded and the young growth will shoot up immediately. Incidentally this young growth supplies excellent cover for all wildlife, and especially good feed for deer. You had better call Skipper again, Sue."

Susan began to call the dog, waiting between calls to get some response. Suddenly Susan said, "Listen. Is that a dog barking?" There was a long silence. "No. I guess not," said Susan. "I'm so afraid for Skipper. What will he do if he's lost out here all night?"

"Don't worry about that, Sue. Dogs have good survival instincts. If he's out here when it gets dark, he'll just wait until he can see again in the morning."

Dick then looked up and to the west. "Darkness is not too far off," he said. "We should be thinking about picking up Tom and getting off the island before it gets too dark.''

He had no sooner spoken than Max appeared coming down the hill he had climbed to view the marsh. "We'd better pack up and move out of here before it gets dark,'' he said. "With that cloud cover moving in it'll come quick tonight. We'll come back in the morning, Susan, and look for Skipper. He'll be all right out here until then. For all we know he could be home already.''

They all returned to the pickup truck and started back. When they reached the fork in the trail, the truck was there with Red, Ira, and Tom standing in front of it.

"I see you didn't find him either,'' Red said. "It looks like he's here for the night then.''

"Looks that way,'' answered the forester. "Hop in, Tom, and we will head home. Red, you and Ira take the lead and we'll follow you out. Thanks for your help.''

"Our pleasure,'' said Ira, as he and Red climbed into their truck. "You'll find your dog, Susan. Don't worry. He'll be okay out here.''

With that the trucks began to make their way off the island.

Chapter 5

HOPE OF TOMORROW

When they got back to the resort, Aunt Martha was on the porch of the lodge wiping her hands on her apron.

"Oh, I see you didn't find him," she said as they walked toward her. "I'm sorry, Susan. You'll find him in the morning though, I'm sure. Max," she continued, "Ralph called. He and Dorothy are going to be late. They said not to wait up for them."

"Supper sure smells good," Max remarked, sniffing the air.

"It's about ready, too," replied Martha. "Won't you stay and have supper with us, Dick? We have more than enough. Baked chicken and everything that goes with it. Apple pie, too."

"Martha, I'd love to, if you're sure I'm not putting you out any," he answered. "I'm batching it tonight. The wife has the children down to Stevens Point visiting her parents. They won't be back until tomorrow afternoon. It was going to be a soup and sandwich night for me."

"Nonsense," said Max. "We're glad to have you. Besides, the way Susan has been talking the arm off you, she probably wants to bend your ear some more before she is through."

"Oh, Uncle Max! I was just asking Mr. Russell about the forests and what he does with them," Susan cried. "I do so love the trees and the animals. I love just everything about the woods. Someday I'd like to work in the forests. Mr. Russell, do you think a girl could ever do the work you do?"

"I don't know why not, Susan!" he answered. "Women are going into most occupations these days. While I don't personally know of any woman foresters, I'm sure there must be some. There are a lot of women already in related work that I know of, such as scientific research, soil conservation, wildlife and fisheries management. They work in state and United States government agencies as well as for private industry. I'll bet by the time you're ready for college there will be many girls going into the forestry services. College is a must for a professional forester, Susan. There is so much you must learn to enter forestry or related conservation fields."

"Is everyone washed up? Dinner's ready and it's being served right now," interrupted Aunt Martha as she placed some covered dishes on the table. "Max, when you come in from the kitchen bring that platter of chicken."

"Is there anything I can do?" asked the forester.

"Not really," replied Aunt Martha. "Just sit down and make yourself feel right at home."

Max brought in the chicken platter and everyone took his seat; Aunt Martha at the end of the rectangular table nearest the kitchen, Max at the opposite end, and Mr. Russell sitting directly across from Tom and Susan.

Uncle Max folded his hands and bowed his head in silent prayer and all followed suit. As they raised their heads, Susan turned to Tom and said, "I asked the Lord to watch over Skipper till he gets home."

"So did I," Tom replied.

You could tell by the big smiles on the faces of the others that it had been a common prayer.

"Say, Dick, I noticed how good that stand of white pine looks on the south end of the marsh. Wasn't that the area that had that blight about four years ago? It really looked bad then," said Max.

"It sure did," Dick answered. "The blight covered most of our land and all of the state's on that end of the island. We had a big crew working on that—State Rangers, U.S. For-

estry Service, plus our people. We had to do some burning where it was really bad. A little select cutting and a complete dusting saved the rest. We haven't seen any sign of that blight in this area since, but they've had a lot of trouble in the New England area the last couple years. They're using the methods we developed here to control it.''

"You mean you have to be a tree doctor too?" asked Tom.

"That's about it. Everything that has to do with our company's forest is my direct responsibility. But I love it. While often it's long, hard work, most of the time I just wonder at the fact that I can be paid well for working with nature as I do. Martha," he added, "this chicken is just delicious. Really, everything is great."

"I'm glad you like it," answered Martha, "But save some room for the apple pie."

After dinner they all went out on the front porch, which overlooked the lake and was completely enclosed by windows. Because the lodge was built into the side of the hill leading down to the lake, the porch was actually a full story above ground level. Susan and Tom excused themselves and went down to the lake to listen for their dog.

Max, Martha, and the forester had chatted for awhile when Susan and Tom returned.

"We're going to bed," Susan announced, "so that we can get up early and start looking for Skipper."

"That's a good idea," said the forester. "I'll go home to bed, too, and be back bright and early to drive you over to the island."

"Boy, that's great!" said Tom. "I hope it will be a good day. Good night everyone."

Susan said her good nights; then she and Tom went to their bedrooms.

"Dick, that's nice of you to come over in the morning, but it's not necessary. Max could go over with the children."

"Martha, I have to be here tomorrow anyway, and besides, Max's pickup is laid up. I wouldn't like to see you take your car over there and get it all scratched up."

"Well, okay, but if you're coming, have breakfast here with us," Martha added.

"Martha," Dick said with a smile, "you're going to spoil me. I'll be here with the dawn." He took Max's hand and said, "See you in the morning." With that, he opened the door and left.

The night was a dark, quiet, windless one, with a sharp chill in the air. The forester buttoned his work shirt collar and as he opened the door to his truck he looked toward the island and said softly, "Hang in there, Skipper. We'll have you home in the morning."

Chapter 6

A MOUTHFUL OF EXPERIENCE

Dawn had hardly brightened the road that led into Trails End Lodge when Dick Russell drove up to Trails End. He stopped his truck next to a blue station wagon which was owned by Susan and Tom's parents. Before he could open his door, Susan and Tom were out of the lodge running towards him.

"Good morning, Mr. Russell," said Tom as he shook his hand. "Aunt Martha's fixing breakfast and we're ready to go to look for Skipper."

"Well, that's fine. Like as not Skipper is up looking for you." He turned to Susan and smiled. "Have a good night's rest, Susan?"

"Not really. I was dreaming of Skipper all night. I hope he's alright," she answered. "Dad and Mother are up, too. Dad would like to go along because Uncle Max has to fix a shower drain."

"Okay with me. Let's go in and meet your parents."

Susan took hold of the forester's hand and half pulled him into the lodge as Tom led the way.

"Mom, Dad, Mr. Russell is here," shouted Tom. "Come and meet him."

Tom and Susan's mother, Dorothy, was the first to enter the room. Her face beamed with a big, warm smile that seemed to brighten the whole room. It was easy to see where Susan got her bubbling personality.

"Mr. Russell," she said, taking his hand. "How very nice to meet you. The children have told me how kind you have been to them, helping them search for Skipper. I do hope they have not been too much trouble. Oh, Ralph, come meet Mr. Russell."

Dorothy had turned toward the kitchen door where a tall man was wiping his hands on a towel. He was dressed in blue jeans and a blue wool shirt. Like his wife's, his smile was as big as the room.

"My pleasure," said the forester as he walked toward him, hand outstretched. "You're just as I imagined. There is no way you could deny Tom was your son. Please call me Dick."

"Dick it is," Ralph Jensen answered. "I hear you gave Susan quite a lesson in forestry. She sure loves nature. But I'm afraid when she gets curious, she never stops asking questions. I hope she wasn't a bother."

"Oh, Dad!" could be heard in the background.

"Don't you believe it, Ralph," the forester said. "I enjoyed every minute."

"Breakfast is ready. The five of you sit down and get to it. Max and I had ours earlier." Martha had just laid down two platters of eggs and sausage. "I'll have the toast out in a jiffy," she said.

"Yes, we should get out to the island as soon as we can. The dog will probably start moving with the light," the forester said as he sat down with the others. "I brought my dog whistle. There's no wind this morning. I thought it might help."

"Susan, don't eat so fast," her mother scolded. "There's time enough to eat properly. Dick, do you think Skipper is still on the island?"

"I think so, Dorothy," he answered. "Like as not he will be trying to backtrack to find his way home. Barring any other distractions, he should come toward any whistle, calling, or noise now that the deer chase has worn off."

After finishing his breakfast, the forester pushed his chair back from the table. "Please excuse me. Before we leave I want to check the radiator of the truck. It was running a little hot on the way here this morning."

"We'll be right with you," Ralph replied. "Susan, Tom, dress warmly now and bring the leash I brought from Ironwood."

When Ralph walked out to the truck, the forester already had the hood up. He was leaning over doing something with both hands.

Ralph looked up at the sky toward the east and then turned toward the west. "It's going to be a beautiful day. Did you find the trouble, Dick?"

"Sure did. The radiator hose was leaking again. I'll have to have it replaced. It's getting a little soft and spongy. Ralph, would you please hand me the five-gallon can from the back of the truck?"

Having added water to the radiator, the forester was just closing the hood of the truck when Tom and Susan ran around the side of the lodge.

"Here's the leash, Dad," Tom said as he climbed into the back seat of the truck.

Susan got in on the driver's side and her father sat in the seat in front of Tom.

"What do you have in the bag, Susan?" her father asked.

"Food for Skipper," she answered. "Aunt Martha thought he'd be hungry when we found him."

The forester had put the water can in the back of the truck. Entering the cab he asked, "Everyone ready?" All answered yes. "Alright then, let's find Skipper." With that he started the engine, backed out, and drove toward Big Island.

When they reached the end of the dike on the island side, the forester stopped the truck. He turned to Tom and said, "Tom, you get out here and watch for Skipper. We'll go up to the fork in the trail, and try to call him in. Once Skipper finds the road I think he'll follow it. But just in case he gets by us up ahead, he'll have to pass you here. If you see him, shout loudly. We'll hear you."

Tom jumped out and the truck slowly made its way to the fork in the trail. The forester, Susan, and her father got out and walked around to the front of the truck.

"Ralph, I think we should split up here. We can

get a good view of the left trail up ahead about
three hundred yards. There's a ridge there, and
one can see the trail for a good half mile from that
point. The best view of the right trail is from right
here. If Skipper can backtrack at all, he should
come from the right where Red and Ira saw him
yesterday. However, if the chase led him across
the other trail, he'll travel that one as soon as he
finds it.''

"Dick, I feel like a hike, so if you don't mind,
I'll go up to the ridge and call Skipper from there.
Susan, do you want to stay here or go with me?''

"If you don't mind, Dad, I'd like to stay here
with Mr. Russell. There are a few things I'd like
to ask him. Besides, Skipper doesn't know him
and might not come when he calls.''

"That's right, Susan. I'll see you both later then. I'm sorry, Dick. It looks like you're in for another session."

"No matter," replied the forester. "I enjoy it. Here, take this whistle with you. It will do more good from up there than from here."

Susan's father took the whistle and with a little wave started up the trail. Susan began calling for Skipper. Suddenly she stopped, grabbed the forester's arm, saying, "What's that funny sound?"

The forester was standing facing the opposite direction, peering at the sky through his binoculars. "Geese," he said. "Canadas on the way home to nest. Aren't they beautiful?"

"And noisy, too," Susan added. "Like me, it seems they like to talk a lot."

The forester looked down at Susan with a warm smile and Susan looked at him and giggled. No one could doubt that they were good friends.

"Three nearly perfect V formations like the chevrons on a buck sergeant, and look, Susan, there's another another flight off to the right."

"Oh, yes! I see them," she replied. "Mr. Russell, why do they fly in those V formations?"

"Well, Susan, it seems when the leader flies through the air, he sets in motion a sort of air turbulence as well as a vacuum to the sides and slightly to the rear. If the next goose flies on either side and to the rear of the lead goose, it will be much easier flying for him. This repeats itself right down the line on either side for as many birds that are in the right position. It's the goose in the lead that has the most work. Because of this, they take turns in the lead. Notice, Susan, how high they fly? That's because they are such huge birds, they must fly where the air is less dense and therefore easier to push through. In fact, sometimes they fly so high they are a danger to airplanes."

"They sure are smart birds," said Susan. "I think they're just wonderful!"

Suddenly Susan began calling Skipper again. Over and over she called, while the forester looked over the terrain with his binoculars.

"Mr. Russell," she said suddenly, "You told me about the people who work in jobs like yours or somewhat like yours. However, these people were always working for either a company, a government, or some university. Doesn't a forester ever work for himself?"

"Oh yes, Susan, they surely do," he answered. "I'm glad you thought of that. Many people who advance in the fields we've talked about go into private business for themselves. For example, many foresters and soil and land conservationists have bought land themselves. They use this land to start nurseries or related projects; they crop the forest land they own on a regular planned basis. Some work as private consultants to other landowners—both private and small commercial owners who can't afford to hire a forester. Some of these private businessmen will also contract out on specific projects to private industry, or government agencies. In fact, most of those people in private business do nearly all of these things I've mentioned."

"That's what I'd like to be," answered Susan. "Have my own business working with and for nature."

"Susan," interrupted the forester, "do you see anything familiar coming down the trail?"

Susan turned and looked where the forester was pointing.

"Skipper, oh, Skipper, come here, boy!" she cried.

As Susan called his name the dog speeded up, running as though his life depended upon it. As he neared Susan, she exclaimed, "Look at his face! It's prickly and swollen. Oh! What happened, boy?"

"Looks like he tangled with a porky," said the forester. "He really got a snoot full of quills. It's no wonder we didn't hear any barking. They look like they've been in there since yesterday."

"What should we do?" asked Susan. "Can we pull out those quills? Oh, you poor dog!"

"We could," answered the forester, "but as tender as his nose and mouth must be by now, we'd better take him to the vet and let him do it. He will give Skipper something to quiet him down and lessen the pain as he pulls the quills out. Get in the truck and hold Skipper. We'll pick up your father and brother and drive to town."

Susan got in the truck and the forester put Skipper on her lap.

"There, there, Skipper," she said. "We're going to fix you up just fine. Oh, Skipper! That must hurt so much. It won't be long now."

Chapter 7

I THOUGHT YOU'D NEVER ASK

The forester drove up the south trail and picked up Susan's father. Then they picked up Tom at the dike and drove to Mercer in about twenty minutes. The veterinarian's office was on Echo Lake on the east end of town. It was constructed of whole logs and stone in such a way that it seemed to blend into the surrounding countryside.

"Do you think the vet is in?" asked Susan as they got to the office door.

"He usually is, Susan," answered the forester. "His home is in the rear of this building, overlooking the lake. Actually, both Doc Ramond and his wife Louise are veterinarians. One or the other is bound to be here."

The forester held the door while Susan, carrying Skipper, followed by her father and Tom, entered. As the forester closed the door, a voice was heard coming from an open door on the other side of the room. "Make yourselves comfortable, friends. I'll be right with you."

Indeed, one could feel quite comfortable in this room. It was furnished in the early American tradition—maple furniture and woven rag rugs. Except for a counter with a desk behind it, it looked just like a living room.

A grey-haired man in a white smock appeared in the open doorway, wiping his hands on a small white towel, and surveyed the group standing in the reception room. Turning to the forester, he said, "Dick, what do we have here?"

The forester introduced everyone and explained what happened. Then Doctor Ramond took Skipper from Susan's arms and held him up in front of him.

"Well, Skipper, it looks as though you've learned a painful lesson. Porcupines just don't like to be fooled with. Now let's see what we can do to fix you up like new. Susan, would you like to come with me and watch?"

"Oh!" she cried. "I don't know if I could stand watching!"

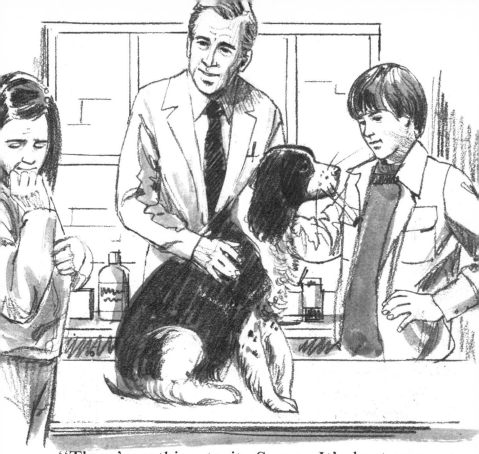

"There's nothing to it, Susan. It's best you watch. Skipper will take it better if you're present. Besides, you should learn how it's done. You may have to do this yourself some day." The veterinarian looked at the others and said, "You can all come back with us. There's no one else here this early. Louise is in Woodruff this morning. You could help me in handling the dog."

They all entered an inner room that was lined with white glassed cabinets. In the center of the room was a large table.

The doctor placed the dog on the table and said, "You hold onto him, Susan, and I'll give him a mild anesthetic." He walked to one of the cabinets and took out a syringe and a small bottle and measured the amount he wanted. "Now, we'll just sterilize the area right here and in we go. There, that wasn't so bad, was it Skipper?" The doctor looked at Susan and said, "That will stop the pain and quiet him down so we can pull the quills."

After a few moments the dog lay down and the doctor stretched him out, his head toward him. "Susan, you and Tom come up here and watch. Dick, if you and Mr. Jensen could hold him steady, just in case he moves, we'll begin. You notice, Susan, some of the quills are smaller than the others. They come from the tail. The rest are from the body and spine of the porcupine. Now both ends of the quills are equally pointed. However, the ends that go into the dog are barbed. When the quills are embedded, like these on the bottom jaw, we must cut the tips off at the other end."

Susan looked at the doctor, ready to ask him a question, when he added, "We cut the tips off because the quill is hollow and full of air. If we squeeze the quill as it is, the air is forced into the end and that extends the barbs, making it very difficult to take them out. With the tip cut off, however, the air is expelled when you squeeze the quill and it comes out easily. You see," he said, holding one up. "On the other hand, when the quills have gone right through the skin, as in the upper lip here, you do not cut off the tips. You merely push the quill right through. Like this!" he said as he held one of those up.

One by one he pulled or pushed the quills out of Skipper. Then he spread a soft salve over the injured parts of the dog's nose and jaw.

"There, that's done, Susan. It wasn't so bad, was it?" he said, smiling at her.

"Oh, no! That was wonderful, Doctor Ramond. I'm so glad you showed Tom and me how to do it," Susan answered. "I'll always remember."

"I knew you would want to learn how quills are removed. Now a little shot of antibiotics and we're through. Susan, take this little envelope of pills with you and give Skipper one a day until they're gone. They'll help prevent any infection."

Susan's father stepped forward and shook the veterinarian's hand and said, "Doctor, thank you for the help you gave Skipper. We all appreciate it. Now how much do we owe you?"

"Well," said the doctor, "with the various medications that comes to twelve dollars."

"Here it is with our thanks," said Mr. Jensen, placing the money in the doctor's hand.

Dick Russell picked Skipper up and turning to Susan, said "Let's get your dog home, Susan." Looking at the doctor, he added, "Thanks, Doc. I'll see you soon."

"Hope so," the doctor replied, with a big smile.

Tom reached over and took the doctor's hand. "Thanks doctor, that was great."

"My pleasure, Tom," he replied. "By the time you get home Skipper should be feeling just fine, except for a tender mouth."

With a laugh they all returned to the truck and drove off.

Having brought Skipper home everyone was standing by the pickup truck saying good-bye. Susan went to the forester's side. Holding his hand, she looked up at him and said, "Mr. Russell, thank you so much for everything. I don't know what we would have done without your help."

There was a short pause and then she added, "We'll be going home Sunday, but we'll be back the fourth of July. Do you suppose we could meet again and you could teach me more about the

woods, nature, and forestry? I would love to see you again.''

The forester looked down and smiled. ''Susan,'' he said, ''I thought you'd never ask. I'm going to look forward to seeing you all again in July. I'll check with Max to see when you'll be up for sure and make arrangements for you, Tom, and anyone else who cares to come along, to visit our paper plant to see how it operates.''

''Isn't that wonderful, Susan?'' her mother said. ''We're so indebted to you.''

''Not at all,'' Dick replied as he climbed into his truck and started the engine. ''I had better get going now and earn my pay. Until I see you again, may God bless you all.''

With a happy wave, he was gone.

Susan looked after him. ''God bless you too, Mr. Russell,'' she said. ''I'll see you in July.''

REFERENCE SECTION

GLOSSARY OF TERMS

back track   Ability to follow one's own trail back to where it started.

blight   Term generally used to describe diseases infecting forests and plant life, starting or stopping growth, and eventually destroying plants or trees.

culvert   The channel opening under the dike, used to pass from one side to the other.

dike   An embankment built to hold back or control water. The top of the embankment can form a causeway.

drag trail   Paths in the forest that are cleared to allow cut timber to be moved to the road or loading site.

flowage   A man-made lake, caused by back waters of a dammed river. Usually the dam is built to provide electric power and/or flood control.

fork (in trail)   Place where a followed road or trail separates into two or more pathways.

hardwood   The wood from trees such as oak, cherry, maple, mahogany used to make or build things.

logging camp	Headquarters usually set up near the center of a forest logging operation. The camp provided housing, meals and medical attention for loggers. It also provided maintenance and storage facilities for equipment and cut timber. Area also included stables for livestock used in logging.
marsh	Wet lands, usually with some standing water. Normally surrounded by higher land causing slow drainage. Most often a basin of a dead lake.
pot holes	The deep holes found in road surfaces usually caused by heavy traffic or severe weather.
pulpwood	The soft wood, often spruce, used to make paper.
ridge	Top of a long stretch of highland. Land drops off sharply on either side. Sometimes a cluster of mountains.
stand	A number of trees of a certain species growing in a given area.
survey crew	Men assigned to assist surveyor set boundary lines and/or layout roads etc. for a logging operation.
tamarack	A tree found in northern United States and Canada. It grows in low flat wetlands. It has needles like pines and other evergreen trees, however, it drops all its needles each fall.
Veterinarian	A doctor, whose practice is limited to diseases and injuries of animals.

For those of you who, like Susan, are interested in forestry or related careers in conservation and ecology, I have compiled the following information. While this data is in no way meant to be complete, I feel it can effectively guide you in exploring this career area.

WHERE TO WRITE FOR ADDITIONAL INFORMATION

Material available is varied and quite extensive. They include career information on forestry, wildlife, and soil conservation subjects as well as forest product development. Material is available for individuals and for classroom study. Ask for catalog or lists when writing.

Forest Service
U. S. Department of Agriculture
Washington, D.C. 20050

American Forestry Association
919-17th St. N.W.
Washington, D.C. 20006

American Forest Institute
1619 Massachusetts Ave. N.W.
Washington, D.C. 20036

PROFESSIONAL CAREERS

Representative positions requiring 4 years of college resulting in a degree in the specific occupational cluster indicated by job title. Some postgraduate training may be required. Experience is required for supervisory positions.

Government
    National Forest Supervisor
    Regional Staff Supervisor
    U.S. District Forest Ranger
    U.S. Forest Ranger
    U.S. Assistant Forest Ranger
    Farm and Service Foresters
    Research Forester
    Also similar positions in state, county and municipalities

Industrial (Private)
  Private Forest Consultant
  Woodlands Manager and Assistants
  Resident Forest Superintendent and Assistants
  Senior Forester
  Forester
  Junior Forester
Related Professions
  Soil and Range Conservationists
  Wildlife and Fisheries Managers
Other professionals working within this occupational cluster.
  Engineers, Surveyors, Chemists, Botanists,
  Entomologists, Geologists, Economists,
  Statisticians, etc.

SUB-PROFESSIONAL OR TECHNICAL CAREERS

Those positions requiring 2 years college or post high school technical
training. Some on-the-job training also is required.

Forestry aides
Timber cruisers
Road survey party chief
Forest workers
Lookouts
Fire dispatchers
Fire control assistants
Research aides
Tree nursery aides
Recreational guards
Smoke chasers
Smoke jumpers
Parachute packers
Administrative and accounting personnel

OTHER OCCUPATIONS

Employment available in jobs not necessarily related to forestry, conservation and ecology. These jobs require varied education and training in the specific skills the job title indicates. These people are employed at hundreds of regional and field offices.

Skilled trades such as:

Mechanics	Machine operators
Electricians	Bulldozer operators
Carpenters	Truck drivers
Cooks	Warehousemen, etc.

Clerical workers such as:

Secretaries	Payroll clerks
Stenographers	File clerks
Typists	Mail clerks, etc.

Woodland semi-skilled and unskilled laborors:

Road and trail crews	Cutting crews
Survey crews	Fire crews, etc.

SCHOOLS

More than 50 colleges and universities offer a professional degree in forestry (4 years or more). A number of these universities offer postgraduate studies toward master and doctorate degrees. There are, in addition, schools offering excellent 1 and 2 year courses in forestry resulting in certificates that are quite satisfactory for entering a sub-professional occupation.

Information on these schools is available from:
Society of American Foresters
1010 16th Street N.W.
Washington, D.C. 20036

Recommended reading:
"So You Want to Be a Forester"
by Charles Edgar Randall

Available from:
The American Forestry Association
919-17th St. N.W.
Washington, D.C. 20006

About the Author:

Richard D. Schwerman has been a business executive and a consultant for more than thirty years. During the last ten years he has concentrated his efforts in the areas of Personnel Administration, human relations, and career guidance. Mr. Schwerman is the co-creator and publisher of the Sextant Series, a profound multi-volume set of career books ranging through all grade levels. He has now turned his efforts toward writing adventure stories. According to Mr. Schwerman, "Life is an adventure, if you let it be, good or bad it is up to you. Careers and adventure belong together." Mr. Schwerman makes his home in Windlake, Wisconsin.

About the Artist:

Richard Wahl, graduate of the Art Center College of Design in Los Angeles, has illustrated a number of magazine articles and booklets. He is a skilled artist and photographer who advocates realistic interpretations of his subjects. He lives with his wife and small son in Evanston, Illinois.